DRE... ...E
RED C......R

CAO XUEQIN

www.realreads.co.uk

Retold by Christine Sun
Illustrated by Shirley Chiang

Published by Real Reads Ltd
Stroud, Gloucestershire, UK
www.realreads.co.uk

Text copyright © Christine Sun 2011
Illustrations copyright © Shirley Chiang 2011
The right of Christine Sun to be identified as
author of this book has been asserted by her in accordance
with the Copyright, Design and Patents Act 1988

First published in 2011

ISBN 978-1-906230-36-4

Printed in Singapore by Imago Ltd
Designed by Lucy Guenot
Typeset by Bookcraft Ltd, Stroud, Gloucestershire

CONTENTS

THE CHARACTERS

Baoyu

Baoyu enjoys the company of girls, and is determined to do all he can to protect them. Can he successfully marry the girl he truly loves?

Daiyu and Baochai

Daiyu is talented and sensitive, while Baochai is capable and considerate. Which of them will win Baoyu's heart?

Yuanchun, Yinchun, Tanchun and Xichun

Each of Baoyu's four sisters has her own story to tell, but what part will they play in Baoyu's life?

Xifeng and Xiangyun

Xifeng is Baoyu's cousin-in-law, in charge of running the household. Xiangyun is Baoyu's second cousin. What can they teach Baoyu?

Miaoyu

Miaoyu is a young and beautiful nun living in a temple sponsored by Baoyu's family. Can she avoid the temptations of worldly affairs?

Qingwen and Xiren

Qingwen and Xiren are Baoyu's maids, taking care of everything in his life and worshipping him as a god. Are they secretly in love with him?

Baoyu's father and mother

Baoyu's father is a scholar and disciplinarian, while his mother is deeply religious. What are their plans for Baoyu's life and loves?

DREAM OF THE RED CHAMBER

Many, many years ago the sky cracked open, water leaked from the heavenly river, and the whole world was flooded. Seeing the people suffering from their loss of homes and crops, the goddess Nuwa decided to mend the sky. She transformed a massive mountain into 36,501 precious stones, and all but one of these she used to mend the hole.

The stone that was left over felt useless and sad.

Near where the stone lay was a lovely red flower growing by the side of a river. The precious stone was fascinated by the delicacy and fragrance of the flower, and devoted himself to caring for her day and night.

Grateful for the stone's kindness, the flower made a vow to herself. 'He waters me and helps me grow, but I have nothing to give him in return. Maybe one day he will be transformed into a man, then I can become human too and follow him. I will repay him with all the tears of gratitude that a girl can weep in a lifetime.'

Many years later, a young girl called Daiyu sat alone in her room and wept. She was sad because her father had become very poor since his wife died, so he had sent her, his only daughter, to live with his mother-in-law, Daiyu's grandmother.

Beautiful and delicate as a flower, Daiyu was often sick. Ever since she was little she had spent a lot of time lying on her bed, feeling useless and sad. Although she wasn't physically strong, she was very creative. She wrote poems and studied music and literature.

Daiyu had just arrived at her new home and hadn't yet met her grandmother. She was worried that her grandmother's large and rich family would look down on her, and that she wouldn't be loved. Would they see beyond her frailty and appreciate her talents?

She was startled by a knock at the door, and it opened to reveal a young man standing in the corridor. He was a little older than her, and looked strangely familiar. It was as if she had known him for a long time, though she was sure they had never met before. He was dressed casually, but every bit of his clothing was of the best quality. His radiant self-confidence was obviously the result of a comfortable life, but he was neither arrogant nor rude.

'Hello, I am Baoyu, your cousin,' he smiled, like an old friend. 'Would you like to come to dinner? Grandma would like everyone to meet you!'

Dining with Baoyu's family was an overwhelming experience for Daiyu. The room was large and lavishly decorated, brimming with antiques and luxuriously scented candles. A group of servants were busy arranging the huge round table in the centre of the room, their footsteps light and well disciplined. Maids were presenting teas and handtowels to the diners. All were handsomely dressed and looked very much at ease with the bustling surroundings.

Daiyu was introduced to the family. Baoyu's grandmother and mother were both very religious, and showered her generously with the Buddha's blessings. Baoyu's father was a stern-looking scholar. He greeted Daiyu politely, but then turned to Baoyu and started questioning him about his studies.

Three pretty girls dressed in similar clothing – Yinchun, Tanchun and Xichun – were introduced as Baoyu's sisters. Daiyu met so many uncles and aunts that she found it hard to remember who was who.

Baoyu's cousin-in-law, Xifeng, arrived late and apologised profusely. She was young but extremely efficient – even bossy – directing the servants and maids with clear orders. 'What a pretty girl you are!' declared Xifeng, holding Daiyu's hands in her own. 'How old are you? What books have you studied? You look so pale! Are you taking any medicine? This is your home now, so just tell me what you want to eat and wear. Let me know if the servants and maids are lazy or careless, and I will deal with them!'

Dinner was served – a plate of nuts to exercise the teeth, a cup of green tea to cleanse the palate, a bowl of ginseng tea to warm the stomach, four plates of sweets to soothe the throat, four plates of savouries to raise the appetite, four larger dishes as main courses, a bowl of soup to calm the stomach, another cup of green tea to rinse the palate, a dish of warm rose water to wash the hands, and, finally, a cup of top-quality jasmine tea and a plate of dumplings to conclude the meal.

'I told them not to cook too much, as I've heard that you don't like rich food,' Xifeng explained to Daiyu. Daiyu smiled as graciously as she knew how.

After dinner, everyone retired to an equally gorgeous room to talk. Sitting next to her grandmother, Daiyu felt quite dizzy that she was now part of this wealthy family. Her father had told her that Baoyu's eldest sister, Yuanchun, was one of the Emperor's favourite concubines. Thanks to this connection, many of Baoyu's relatives were promoted to high power, and the whole family had become prosperous. Daiyu tried to imagine what life in the royal palace would be like. Yuanchun must be very happy.

Suddenly Baoyu's face was in front of her. 'Where is your precious stone?' he asked.

'What?' Daiyu was surprised out of her thoughts. 'What are you talking about?'

'Here, look at mine.' Baoyu dragged a gold necklace out of his collars and showed her the emerald gemstone attached to it. Reflecting the bright candlelight, it was as though the stone held some ancient and long-forgotten promise.

'Nice, isn't it?' Baoyu said unceremoniously. 'People say I was born with this stone in my mouth. I'm surprised I didn't choke to death! How big can a baby's mouth be? Where is yours?'

Daiyu was embarrassed. 'I haven't got one,' she answered stiffly. 'Not everyone is fortunate enough to have such a rare gemstone.'

Baoyu was suddenly angry, and his face turned white. He pulled the necklace from his neck and threw it to the floor, the gold thread cutting his flesh. He stamped on it, shouting, 'What do you mean, rare? Who wants this piece of junk anyway!'

Xiren, Baoyu's maid, threw herself to the floor to protect the precious stone from her master's violent feet. Baoyu's grandmother shouted, 'What do you think you're doing, destroying something so precious!' Concerned that the old lady was about to have a heart attack, Xifeng instructed a servant to fetch the family doctor as quickly as possible.

Baoyu burst into tears. 'What good is the stone anyway? My sisters, cousins and nieces don't have stones. Even Daiyu doesn't have one. It must be bad to have a stone!'

Seeing the desperation in Baoyu's eyes, Daiyu quickly said, 'I – I used to have one. It's just that when my mother died my father decided to bury my precious stone with her, so that part of me would always be with her.' Though she knew it was a story made up to comfort Baoyu, it made Daiyu sad, and she was nearly in tears herself.

'Oh, please don't cry!' Baoyu pleaded. 'I'll be sad if you cry.' He immediately forgot all about his own troubles. By the time Xiren put the gold necklace with its precious stone back round his neck, Baoyu was already telling Daiyu jokes to cheer her up.

The next day Daiyu was invited to Baoyu's study, where he and a group of girls were discussing poetry. Apart from Baoyu's three sisters – Yinchun, Tanchun and Xichun – four other girls were present. Two of them were Baoyu's maids, Xiren and Qingwen.

Daiyu was introduced to Xiangyun, Baoyu's second cousin, who was dressed like a handsome young man. She also ate and drank like a man, enjoying wine and barbequed pork while the other girls fussed about their trim waistlines.

'Come and sit with me, beautiful girl,' said Xiangyun to Daiyu. 'I want to find out why Baoyu likes you so much.' As the two girls sat and chatted together, Daiyu felt immediately attracted to Xiangyun's honesty and cheerfulness.

Miaoyu, on the other hand, seemed distant and cold. Daiyu was surprised to find that she was a Buddhist nun living and studying in the ancestral hall of Baoyu's family. While the other girls picked happily through the snacks prepared by Qingwen and Xiren, Miaoyu sat wiping her fingers repetitively as if she was worried that she might catch other people's germs. There was something about the nun that reminded Daiyu of her own loneliness and desire to seek friends.

Baoyu was asking everyone what they thought about a poem that described girls as dazzling butterflies. 'I disagree with the poet, because butterflies are common and ordinary,' he said.

'I like butterflies,' Yinchun said, 'they are beautiful and energetic.'

'Of course you like them,' Tanchun immediately challenged her sister, 'but what you forget is that butterflies live for just one day.'

'Stop picking on her,' Xichun quickly intervened. She was always the one who kept the peace. 'Not everyone is as clever and knowledgeable as you.'

'What do you think, Xiren and Qingwen?'
Xiangyun asked the maids. She treated
them as equals and knew that they too were
intelligent and well-read.

'I don't know much about poetry,' Xiren
answered humbly, 'but I think butterflies are
lucky because they can always find flowers to
rest upon.'

Xiangyun nodded, but Qingwen sneered.
'Come on, Xiren. You're thinking that our
young master Baoyu should only study
serious books and forget about these romantic
poems.'

Everybody laughed. Then Miaoyu said,
'You all seem to forget that even though
butterflies are beautiful, it is up to mother
nature to decide their fate. While the
lucky ones may be able to rest on flowers,
unfortunate butterflies die like fallen leaves.'

When she heard this Daiyu suddenly
felt a chill down her spine, as if Miaoyu had
foreseen something ominous.

'Whatever you say,' said Baoyu, looking admiringly round the circle of girls, 'I disagree with the poet because I think girls are as pure as water. Men like me are as dirty as mud. Men are morally and spiritually inferior to women, and girls in particular should be well protected and worshipped by those around them.'

A few days later another girl arrived in Baoyu's family. Baochai was a cousin of Baoyu's, and had come for a long visit. She had a round, intelligent face, fair skin and large eyes, and in sharp contrast with Daiyu's frailty she was fit and healthy.

At the family dinner, Baochai immediately won everyone's heart. Baoyu's grandmother liked her pleasant manners, while Baoyu's father and mother praised her broad knowledge in Buddhist teachings. Xifeng loudly complimented her sensible and tactful ways of handling the servants and maids, as they obviously respected her and willingly rushed to fulfil her every wish. Even Baoyu's three sisters admired her modest nature, as they secretly discussed how confident Baochai looked even in a simple dress and hardly any jewellery.

'What's that around your neck?' Xiangyun asked in her usual straightforward manner. 'Is it a golden locket?'

'Yes,' Baochai answered with a smile, taking off the locket to show everyone. 'It was given to me by a Buddhist monk when I was little. My parents think it'll bring good luck.'

'Look,' said Yinchun. 'There are words engraved on it, just like on Baoyu's precious stone.'

Everyone had a closer look. While Baoyu's emerald green gemstone was inscribed 'Don't lose or forget me, and I will sustain and enrich you', the inscription on Baochai's golden locket read, 'Don't leave or abandon me, and I will keep you young forever'.

19

'How amazing!' exclaimed Xifeng. 'It's almost as though Baoyu's stone and Baochai's locket are a magic pair!' She turned to Daiyu, who had said nothing. 'What do you think, Daiyu? Isn't this incredible? It's almost like destiny!'

Daiyu nodded, but found it hard to concentrate. She looked at Baoyu, who smiled warmly and rolled his eyes as if to say 'Here they go again – it's only a stone and a locket'. But she couldn't help feeling that something had come between them.

Life in Baoyu's family carried on peacefully. Baoyu and Daiyu spent every day in each other's company, sometimes arguing over silly things but most of the time studying and playing chess together happily. Yinchun, Tanchun and Xichun were their best friends, and Xiangyun and Baochai were often there too. Miaoyu was with them less often, but Daiyu enjoyed her company whenever she was there.

Before long it was the annual Lantern Festival and, as she did every year, Baoyu's sister Yuanchun arranged to visit her old home. As one of the Emperor's favourite concubines, Yuanchun arrived with hundreds of palace guards and servants. Everyone in Baoyu's family, from his grandmother and parents to all the servants, got down on their knees to welcome her. Dressed in a brilliant silk gown decorated with golden phoenixes, Yuanchun graciously received their good wishes. She then passed on the Emperor's greetings and distributed gifts to everyone present.

When the public ceremony was over, Yuanchun spent time with her family and a handful of her closest guards. As she sat with her parents, grandmother, brother and sisters Yuanchun wanted so desperately to be a young, innocent, carefree daughter again. She sighed, and the tears slid down her cheeks. Yuanchun's family wanted so much to hold her in their arms, but as commoners they dared not touch the Emperor's concubine.

Soon Yuanchun had to go back to the palace. She looked back briefly at her beloved family as her guards jostled her out of the door. She told them to take care and promised to come back next year, then she was gone.

Daiyu thought she had never seen anybody looking so lost and lonely.

After Yuanchun's visit, Daiyu felt very depressed. One day, as she walked in the garden, she saw that the ground was littered with fallen flowers,

some still fresh and colourful, some dry and withered. Taking pity on the half-dead flowers, she took a shovel and tried to bury them. She knew people would think her silly if they saw her doing this, but she simply couldn't help it. She wondered who would bury her when it was her turn to die, and burst into tears.

Baoyu was on his way to visit Daiyu when he heard her crying. It reminded him of the mother she had lost, and how she depended on someone else's family to survive. It made him wonder about his own family's fortunes. What would happen if his family became poor? Where would he go if he lost his family?

The next day, Baoyu's grandmother went to the temple to pray for heaven's blessings. After she had prayed, she was talking with the temple official, who enquired after the health of her family. He remarked jokingly that Baoyu was now old enough to get married, and wouldn't Baoyu's precious stone and Baochai's golden locket be the best engagement presents the young couple could possibly give to one another? His remarks were soon passed round everyone in Baoyu's family.

A few days later Daiyu was feeling unwell, and was resting in her room when Baoyu's two maids, Qingwen and Xiren, came to see her. Assuming that Daiyu was asleep, the maids turned to leave. But Daiyu was awake and could hear every word they were saying.

'Daiyu had better give up that silly dream of hers,' said Xiren.

'Yes, Baoyu will never be able to marry her,' replied Qingwen, 'his family wouldn't allow it.'

'Our young master might marry me,' Xiren answered. 'Baoyu is always nice to me – I'm his favourite.'

'You haven't a chance. You know how much Baoyu likes Daiyu,' giggled Qingwen, 'and his family likes Baochai. Both girls are a thousand times better than you are – you're just a maid.'

'Just you wait and see!' replied Xiren angrily as the two maids disappeared down the corridor.

What she had heard left Daiyu in despair. How could she, a poor and sickly orphan, compete against Baochai, who not only was healthy and beautiful but had captured the hearts of everyone in Baoyu's family?

Daiyu wasn't the only one with problems. For years the efficient Xifeng, Baoyu's cousin-in-law, had been in charge of the family's financial affairs. In order to increase the family's assets, she had taken in many poor relatives and acquired their land. These relatives needed to be fed and clothed and their land farmed and harvested, all of which required money. And the money was fast running out.

It didn't help that several family members had enjoyed their luxurious life so much that they became arrogant and abusive. One used his power to coerce the daughter of a poor neighbour into becoming his concubine; another forcibly shut down a local antique shop in order to obtain a priceless Ming vase. Yet another got drunk and ordered his servants to beat up a farmer who dared to argue with him in the market. All of these troubles required money to settle.

To make matters even worse, Xifeng discovered that her husband was having an affair with a maid. She immediately sacked the maid, who soon committed suicide in shame. She then confronted her husband, demanding an apology, but he refused. She felt humiliated by her husband's adultery, and was angry that he wouldn't apologise, but she still had to put on a brave face in front of her family.

The pressure was too much for Xifeng; she became ill, and Tanchun took over the family's financial affairs. Although she was young and inexperienced, Tanchun managed to reduce expenses by retiring those servants who were too old to work. She stopped giving the maids pocket money for new dresses and jewellery.

She even learned book-keeping and caught the accountant stealing to subsidise his drinking.

While most of Baoyu's family admired Tanchun's management skills, there were some who resented her for their loss of privileges and financial favours. They sought every opportunity to bad-mouth Tanchun in front of Baoyu and Tanchun's grandmother and parents.

As Xifeng's health recovered she tried to take back control of the family's finances. Using the excuse that an important piece of family jewellery was missing, she ordered a search of the personal belongings of all the servants and maids, making it clear that if anything were found it would reflect very badly on that person's master or mistress.

Tanchun's maids were the first to be searched, but Tanchun stood up for them and stoutly defended their innocence. When one of Xifeng's servants tried to search Tanchun's own things, she slapped the servant's face and accused him of disrespect.

Then one of Xichun's maids was accused of hoarding money, and one of Yinchun's maids was found to be having an affair with another servant. Both maids were sacked, and Xichun and Yinchun felt harassed and humiliated.

Then Baoyu's maid Qingwen was searched. Nothing was found, but Xifeng had long disliked Qingwen's sharp tongue and wanted this chance to get rid of her. She insisted the maid should be dismissed, using the excuse of protecting Baoyu's innocence. 'She's good-looking and stays with her young master day and night,' said Xifeng righteously. 'I wouldn't be at all surprised if she tried to seduce Baoyu.'

Qingwen was sacked and sent away. Before long she fell sick and died. Baoyu was grief-stricken. Unable to ease his sorrow, he tried to imagine Qingwen as the goddess of the peony, happy in heaven.

Baoyu cherished all the girls in his life, and was determined to do all he could to protect them, but it was hard work. The next challenge came when his sister Yinchun was married to the son of a rich local family.

Soon after the wedding Yinchun discovered that her husband loved drinking, gambling, and chasing after beautiful girls, including all their maids. He was abusive and would often beat her. When she confronted him, he claimed that Yinchun's parents had married her to him for his family's money, so there was no reason at all why he should care about her happiness.

Baoyu was worried about his sister's welfare, and spoke to his mother about his concern. 'We need to dissolve Yinchun's marriage and bring her home,' he said. 'Yinchun is the nicest girl in the world. How can anyone stand the cruelty she is now suffering?'

Baoyu's mother sighed. 'A married girl is like spilt milk. What's the use of anyone crying over it? Yinchun now belongs to another family, and there's nothing we can do about it. A woman must be content with the man she marries, no matter what he becomes.'

Baoyu had heard all this before, but he still felt deeply worried about his precious sister Yinchun. Why must girls get married when they grow up? he asked himself. Why can't they be allowed to remain innocent and happy?

However, Baoyu was not the only one concerned about Yinchun. Daiyu was so worried about her that she fell ill, and began to cough blood. Xichun, Tanchun and Xiangyun

were all worried about her symptoms, but Daiyu insisted that nothing about her sickness should be revealed to Baoyu. 'He is under quite enough pressure already,' she told them.

One day, one of Baoyu's uncles was drinking at a local inn. He was a vain man and always needed to know better than anyone else. He complained that the wine tasted bad, and when the innkeeper came over to see what the fuss was about, he started shouting and punched the innkeeper repeatedly. By the time Baoyu's uncle could be pulled off the poor man, the innkeeper was dead.

Baoyu's uncle was arrested and thrown into jail, but Xifeng came to his rescue. She paid a huge bribe to the judge, who promptly declared that the killing was an accident and set Baoyu's uncle free. Everyone involved in the case, including the waiters at the inn and the guards at the jail, was given money to keep them quiet.

Baoyu's parents decided that something joyous and festive would help everyone forget the family's problems and start bringing good luck instead of misfortune and embarrassment. Maybe a wedding would help rescue the family and restore the proper order of things. Bayou was the obvious candidate. He was spending too much time with the girls, and marriage would help him grow up. But who should he marry?

After some thought, they chose Baochai, always healthy, polite and obedient. And surely the inscriptions on Baochai's golden locket and Baoyu's emerald gemstone indicated that the wedding was blessed by the heavens.

Although the decision wasn't formally announced, everyone in the family soon knew that Baoyu was getting married, and who he was getting married to. But the announcement did not reverse the family's fortunes, and it wasn't long before two more tragedies struck.

The first was the loss of Baoyu's precious gemstone. Baoyu himself seemed unmoved by the loss – he said that he took it off to get changed one day and simply forgot about it when he was dressed. As he had never considered the stone very important, losing it didn't bother him much.

Though the stone wasn't important to Baoyu, his parents panicked and ordered a thorough search of everyone's belongings. Every inch of the family land was carefully searched and all the rooms, even the toilets, were checked, but the stone wasn't anywhere to be found.

Then the family was notified that Yuanchun, their noble daughter and the Emperor's favourite concubine, had died suddenly. Baoyu's grandmother and parents hurried to the palace to participate in the state funeral, and everyone in the family was kept busy as condolences were received from relatives and friends near and far.

Amidst all this chaos Baoyu sank deeper and deeper into himself, and appeared to lose all interest in what was happening around him. He lost interest in food, found it hard to sleep, and stopped talking to anyone. Day after day he sat in the garden, occasionally smiling to himself and looking wistfully at the flowers.

'It's all because he's lost his precious stone, which is his soul!' Baoyu's grandmother insisted. Baoyu's parents announced a huge reward for anyone who could locate the stone, but to no avail. 'Let's get Baoyu and Baochai married,' Baoyu's grandmother ordered, desperately resorting to the common belief that a healthy wife would benefit the soul and body of her husband. 'The sooner it is done, the sooner we can save Baoyu's life.'

Xiren had her own idea about why her young master was acting so oddly. She knew that Baoyu and Daiyu loved each other dearly, even though they had never revealed this to each other or anybody else.

Xiren told Baoyu's mother of her concern. On behalf of her young master, who seemed to have no idea of what was going on around him, she begged Baoyu's mother to consider the possibility of Baoyu marrying Daiyu. 'If Baoyu marries Baochai instead of Daiyu, then I'm afraid he will go completely crazy!' she cried.

Baoyu's mother refused to believe Xiren. She went straight to consult the devious Xifeng, who quickly devised a plan. Soon almost everyone in the family was busy organising Baoyu and Baochai's wedding – Baoyu, Baochai and Daiyu, however, were all kept completely in the dark about the plans.

A few days later Daiyu found one of the maids crying in the garden. When Daiyu asked what had happened, the maid said she had been beaten by the other servants for saying something wrong.

'What did you say that made the others so angry?' asked Daiyu.

'I said that it's wonderful that our young master Baoyu will soon marry Baochai,' the maid explained innocently. 'They told me not to talk about it, but why should we hide such great news? I even heard that Baoyu's parents are planning to find you a nice husband!'

Daiyu was stunned. She felt her heart miss a beat, and it seemed as though she had lost all the strength in her body. She dismissed the maid and wandered alone through the garden, not knowing where to go or what to do. She felt that she was fighting single-handedly against the whole world. Everyone despised her. They couldn't wait to get rid of her.

'I know,' said Daiyu to herself, suddenly knowing what she needed to do. 'I'll go and ask Baoyu. If he loves Baochai instead of me, I need to hear the words from him.'

When she arrived at Baoyu's room, all he could do was smile weakly at her. She smiled back, unsure of what to say. Was it right to bother Baoyu when he looked so ill? Perhaps he would be happier and healthier without her.

'Why have you become so sick, Baoyu?' she asked.

Baoyu answered, 'I am sick for you, Daiyu.'

A smile appeared on Daiyu's pale face. She stood up quietly and returned to her own room. Then she fainted.

All the emotions of the last few days were
too much for Daiyu and she became very ill
again, and could not leave her room. Xifeng
took the opportunity to fulfil her plans. She
presented Baoyu to his parents, and in front
of them she asked, 'Why don't you tell your
parents how happy you are that you are getting
married, Baoyu?' The ever-smiling Baoyu
could think only of Daiyu. 'Yes, I am so happy,'
he answered, remembering Daiyu's pale smile.

His parents, seeing his smile, believed that he was thinking of Baochai.

The deceitful Xifeng took Baoyu aside and said, 'If you're so happy that Daiyu will be your wife you need to start eating and talking to people again. You need to behave like a normal person, otherwise Daiyu will not want to marry you.'

Baoyu's mind suddenly cleared. 'I am normal,' he told Xifeng. 'You're the one that's stupid. There's nothing for Daiyu to worry about. I've already given my heart to her. As soon as she's my wife, she'll give me hers and we shall be as one.'

Xifeng now ordered the family to speed up preparations for Baoyu and Baochai's wedding. 'And do remember to stay away from Daiyu's room,' she told everyone. 'She is not well and must not be disturbed.'

When Daiyu died that same evening, crying Baoyu's name over and over again, there was no one there to comfort her. Everyone was in the great hall, happily celebrating the wedding that was about to take place.

Baoyu still believed he was about to marry Daiyu, and had recovered rapidly. He stood proudly in the great hall in a luxurious robe, a huge smile on his face, watching his bride being led towards him. She was dressed in a stunning red gown embroidered with golden phoenixes. As was the custom, a red scarf covered her face until the moment she was to be revealed to her new husband.

It was only when the groom and bride were pronounced husband and wife that Baoyu was allowed to take the red scarf from his bride's face. He could not believe what he saw. Standing in front of him, her cheeks turning rosy pink because she was both nervous and shy, her big eyes gazing straight at him, her fair skin looking almost transparent under the bright light in the hall, was Baochai.

Baoyu, in a state of complete shock, stood and stared. Where was Daiyu? Where was the girl he truly desired? He turned and ran from the hall.

It appeared to everyone present that Baoyu had lost his mind again. He tried to go to Daiyu's room, and couldn't understand why everyone stopped him. He kept asking for Daiyu, but nobody would give him an answer. He was taken back to his room, and almost immediately fell into a coma.

When Baoyu came out of his coma he was so ill that he could not eat or drink, and did not seem to recognise anybody. All he did was ask to see Daiyu. Many doctors came to examine him, but none could find what was wrong.

'I don't care about her sickness. She's going to die, and I too shall die soon!' Baoyu shouted repeatedly. 'Why don't you put the two of us side by side, so we can die together?'

Baochai decided she had to tell her husband that Daiyu was already dead. She knelt by his bedside and told him about Daiyu as gently as she knew how. 'Is she really gone?' he asked weakly, not really wanting to know the answer.

'Yes, she's dead,' Baochai answered firmly.
'But you are still alive. And you should remain
alive, for the sake of your grandmother and
parents.'

Slowly and painfully Baoyu learned to accept the
loss of his beloved Daiyu. He often thought and
dreamed about her, but he didn't want anyone
to see his tears. He understood that he was now
a married man, and that his wife and family
expected him to be healthy and strong. It was his
responsibility to look forward, not to look back.

But there was not much to look forward
to. He heard that his sister Tanchun was to be
married to the son of a government official. While
the marriage would no doubt benefit the family
and the career of Baoyu's father, it would take
Tanchun far away from home.

When Baoyu heard the news he wept bitterly.
'All the girls I love are now either dead or leaving,'
Baoyu wailed. 'Daiyu and Yuanchun have died.

Yinchun has married a wicked husband and her life is hell. Now Tanchun is leaving, and I expect Xiangyun will soon get married and leave too. I care so much about them all, and they're all taken away from me.'

Baochai heard Baoyu's pain; she felt sad that she seemed less important to him than all those who had gone away, but did her best to comfort him.

Everyone prayed that Tanchun's marriage would be a happy one. They hoped that it would bring good luck to Baoyu's family, which had been increasingly ignored by the Emperor since Yuanchun's death.

The family was running out of money. All those friends and relatives who couldn't wait to build connections with the family when it was rich were now deserting it, like rats abandoning a slowly sinking ship.

To make matters even worse, the bribe arranged by Xifeng to free Baoyu's uncle from the murder charge was now discovered. The Emperor was outraged. He ordered that Baoyu's uncle should be executed and the corrupt judge jailed for life. He instructed that everything belonging to the family should be confiscated as a punishment for interfering with the justice system. The Emperor was determined to prove to his subjects that he would not show favouritism towards anybody that broke the law, not even the relatives of his beloved concubine.

The imperial troops arrived to take everything away, the precious antiques and scented candles, the huge round dining table, the pots, pans, dishes and cutlery, the furniture and ornaments, the cash, the signed and unsigned cheques, the land titles, the jewellery, the clothing and personal belongings of every family member, servant and maid, even the decorated staff that Baoyu's grandmother used to walk with. All that was left were the clothes they stood in.

Xifeng knew all too well that it was her conniving and lying that had brought such disgrace and tragedy to the family. Everything started spinning around her, and she fell to the floor in a dead faint.

Now the family had to leave their fine home and they all moved to somewhere much smaller.

Xiangyun's marriage brought a little light into this time of misery and chaos. Although Baoyu's family now had no money to pay for a proper ceremony, Xiangyun's husband-to-be appeared not to mind, and did his best to look after his wife's relatives and friends.

The marriage seemed a happy one, and news soon arrived that Xiangun was going to have a baby. Everyone in Baoyu's family was thrilled to hear this news, but Baoyu felt as though he had lost something important. Why do girls have to grow up, get married, and have babies, he wondered, as so often before. How he wished they could stay young and innocent forever.

Baoyu thought of Daiyu, who never had the chance to get married and have babies. He thought of Baochai, to whom he had nothing to give. He cried bitterly.

Then came alarming news about Yinchun and her abusive husband. Baoyu's family knew that her husband had treated her like a slave since the day they were married, but they now heard that she had been beaten so badly that she was unlikely to survive his latest attack. Much as they would like to bring her home, they now had neither the money nor the power to do so. When Yinchun died, she was buried hastily by her husband's family, without even a proper funeral.

Baoyu's grandmother was so distraught by Yinchun's death that she lost the will to live, and within days she too was dead. Xifeng felt an overwhelming sense of guilt, and determined to organise a grand funeral, but there was no money, and none of the family's numerous relatives and friends were willing to help her. As a result, the funeral of Baoyu's grandmother was a miserable event. Xifeng remembered how wealthy the family had once been, and how she used to command that wealth as a queen controls her realm. She broke down and wept.

It fell to the Buddhist nun Miaoyu to pray for
heavenly blessings for Baoyu's grandmother
and his sister Yinchun. At night she stayed in
Xichun's room to keep her company. It was
almost like the old days when the girls in Baoyu's
family enjoyed chatting, playing chess and
discussing poetry.

However, the family's misfortunes were not
yet at an end, and one night bandits broke into
the small house where Baoyu's family were now
living. They looted everything they could find, and
threatened to kill the whole family if they dared
to inform the police. As they left they grabbed
Miaoyu, and disappeared into the darkness.

Miaoyu's body was found the next day, and Baoyu's family found it hard to believe how much misfortune they were being made to bear. Was Miaoyu assaulted and killed by the bandits, or did she kill herself to protect her innocence? No one knew, and the uncertainty added to their woes.

Xichun felt there was no longer anything worth living for in this mundane world. Her grandmother, her friend Daiyu, and her sisters Yuanchun and Yinchun were dead, her brother Baoyu and his wife Baochai were a loveless couple, her cousin-in-law Xifeng was ill, and her friend Miaoyu had probably been raped and murdered by the bandits. Although Xiangyun seemed happy, it was rumoured that her husband had incurable tuberculosis. Everyone was suffering.

Perhaps the spiritual life would offer some solace. Xichun found a pair of scissors and cut off her hair. She determined to devote herself to Buddhism and become a nun.

Baoyu never fully recovered from the loss of Daiyu. As everyone he loved drifted away, he began to lose hope, just as his sister Xichun had done. All the beautiful girls in his life had died or left. Only he, a man who felt as dirty as mud, was still there. He had always worshipped his beloved girls, who to him were as pure as water, but he had failed to protect them.

Baoyu dreamed often, and in one dream he found himself in a garden full of beautiful flowers. They nodded and smiled at him, and he seemed to recall once being one of them. He looked at their faces and remembered how close and happy they all used to be.

In the centre of a garden was a wonderful red flower behind a white fence. He tried to reach out and touch it, but an army of ghosts and monsters appeared and chased him away. Desperately he cried out for help.

Baochai and the maid Xiren heard Baoyu calling and ran to him. They told him that just before they heard his cries, a Buddhist monk and a Taoist priest had arrived and asked to meet Baoyu. The two men said they were there to return the precious emerald that Baoyu had lost so long ago. They were waiting for Baoyu in front of the house.

As he made his way to meet them, Baoyu came upon his sister Xichun, now a Buddhist nun. He took her hands and asked her how she was.

'I'm fine,' she said with a smile. 'And how are you?' she asked, surprised at how serene he seemed.

'I'm fine. Really good.' Baoyu smiled too.

Baoyu went out to meet the monk and priest. They gave him his precious stone, which he gladly accepted. Then the three men walked away from the house together. Nobody knows what the monk and priest said to Baoyu. But he was never seen again.

Although Baochai was very sad, she knew she should remain strong in order to look after the rest of the family, especially Baoyu's parents. She imagined Baoyu as an immortal in a heavenly place, perhaps at the foot of a mountain with a lovely river nearby. She prayed that he would finally be happy.

Xiren married one of Baoyu's friends and they had a happy life together. She and her husband often talked about Baoyu, how he loved all the girls in his life and tried to look after them.

Many years later a travelling scholar was resting by a river. He noticed a piece of emerald stone on the riverbank, and when he looked more closely he saw that it had words engraved on it. The scholar decided to write the story down, and it eventually became the book about the dream of the red chamber.

The emerald stone remains by the river, quietly remembering all it has lived through. And the stone doesn't mind whether you believe its story or not, for it is just a story, like a dream that is quickly forgotten when you wake up. If any trace of a dream brings a smile to your face, that will be enough, won't it?

TAKING THINGS FURTHER

The real read

The *Real Reads* version of *Dream of the Red Chamber* is a retelling in English of Cao Xueqin's magnificent (and very long!) Chinese work. If you would like to read the full Chinese version in all its original splendour, you will need to learn the Chinese language. Otherwise you will have to rely on the English translation, details of which can be found on page 61.

Filling in the spaces

The loss of so many Cao Xueqin's original words is a sad but necessary part of the shortening process. We have had to make some difficult decisions, omitting subplots and characters, some important, some less so, but all interesting. We have also, at times, taken the liberty of combining two events into one, or of giving a character words or actions that originally belong to another. The points below will fill in some of the gaps, but nothing can beat the original.

- Baoyu's surname is Jia, which is pronounced the same as the Chinese character 'jia', meaning false, fake or fictitious. This is an important clue provided by Cao for us to understand the portrayal of Baoyu's family as both a realistic description and as a fictional (or 'dream') version of Cao's own family. Cao writes in the first chapter of the full version that his book is intended to be a memorial to the women he knew in his youth, including friends, relatives and maids.

- The book provides a comprehensive record of two branches of Baoyu's family, who live in two large adjacent family compounds in the capital. Numerous pages are devoted to describing the appearances and mannerisms of the characters, as well as their surroundings, daily gatherings, and all kinds of literary activities. Depictions of other aspects of traditional Chinese culture are provided, including medicine, cooking, proverbs, mythology, music, painting, landscaping, matchmaking and courtship.

- There are two 'standard' versions of the book, the original 80 chapters written by Cao and an extended version of 120 chapters, with 40 additional chapters written later by Gao E and Cheng Weiyan. Many other Chinese authors have written their own alternative endings. Cao's original book includes many fine and grand sections written as poetry.

- The full version of the book contains thirty major characters and more than four hundred minor ones, most of whom are female. While women are often portrayed to be more capable and loveable than their male counterparts, there are many more tales of power struggles, hatred, jealousy, conspiracy and even cold-blooded murder than those that are told in this shortened version.

Back in time

Cao Xueqin wrote *Dream of the Red Chamber* in the mid-eighteenth century. Commonly acknowledged as the highest peak of classic Chinese writing, the book is remarkable both for its huge cast of characters and for its detailed description of the life and social structures of the Chinese aristocracy of the time, especially the women. The 'red chamber' of the title refers to the rooms – often painted red – where the daughters of wealthy families lived.

In the book, despite Baoyu's attempt to protect the girls around him, most of them are married off or sold to other wealthy houses and subsequently suffer from violence, neglect and abuse. This reflects both Baoyu's inability to cope with life's harsh realities and his family's gradual decline in power and glory.

To a large extent, Baoyu's fiery passion for love and beauty reflects Cao's life as a highly intelligent and talented artist. In the same way that Baoyu's family slowly loses its fame and fortune, Cao's family properties were confiscated by the government of his time, forcing him to live in poverty. It is clear that *Dream of the Red Chamber* is a semi-autobiographical work, a literary tribute to all the important women in Cao's life.

Finding out more

We recommend the following English books and websites to gain a greater understanding of Cao Xueqin and his writing:

Books

- David Hawkes (and Cao Xuequin), *The Story of the Stone* (in 3 volumes), Penguin Classics, 2006. *The Story of the Stone* is the alternative title of *Dream of the Red Chamber*, and this is the best full-length English translation. It includes the additional forty chapters by Gao E and Cheng Weiyan.

- Dore J. Levy, *Ideal and Actual in The Story of the Stone*, Columbia University Press, 1999. A good introduction for first-time readers of *Dream of the Red Chamber*.

- Anthony C. Yu, *Rereading the Stone: Desire and the Making of Fiction in 'Dream of the Red Chamber'*, Princeton University Press, 2001. Another good introduction for first-time readers.

Website

- www.cliffsnotes.com/WileyCDA/LitNote/
Dream-of-the-Red-Chamber.id-92,pageNum-2.html
Notes on *Dream of the Red Chamber* by Cliffs
Notes, including book introduction, chapter
summary and analysis, Cao Xueqin's biography,
critical essays, and study help.

Food for thought

Here are some things to think about if you are
reading *Dream of the Red Chamber* alone, or ideas
for discussion if you are reading it with friends.
In retelling *Dream of the Red Chamber* we have
tried to recreate, as accurately as possible, Cao
Xueqin's original plot and characters. We have also
tried to imitate aspects of his style. Remember,
however, that this is not the original work;
thinking about the points below, therefore, can
help you begin to understand Cao Xueqin's craft.
To move forward from here, turn to the full-length
English translation of *Dream of the Red Chamber*
and lose yourself in his wonderful storytelling.

Starting points

- Do you agree with Baoyu that girls are as pure as water and should be protected by those around them?

- Do you think parents always know what is the best for their children? Does your view change as you read on? How?

- If Cao Xueqin was writing today, what do you think Baoyu and the girls in *Dream of the Red Chamber* could do to make their lives better and themselves happier?

Themes

What do you think Cao Xueqin is saying about the following themes in *Dream of the Red Chamber*?

- love

- responsibility

- women's status within the family and within society

Style

Can you find paragraphs in *Dream of the Red Chamber* that contain examples of the following?

● descriptions of setting and atmosphere

● the writer allowing the reader to know more than a character knows

● short sentences that express strong feelings being felt by one of the characters

Look closely at how these paragraphs are written. What do you notice? Can you write a paragraph in the same style?

To give you an idea of what Baoyu's house might have looked like, here is an illustration for *Dream of the Red Chamber* by the Chinese artist Sun Wen, painted in the mid-nineteenth century.